Pony-Crazed Princess

Princess Ellie Takes Charge

Read all the adventures of Princess Ellie!

#1 Princess Ellie to the Rescue

#2 Princess Ellie's Secret

#3 Princess Ellie's Mystery

#4 Princess Ellie's Starlight Adventure

#5 Princess Ellie's Camping Trip

#6 A Surprise for Princess Ellie

#7 Princess Ellie Takes Charge

Super Special: Princess Ellie's Summer Vacation

Pony-Crazed Princess

Princess Ellie Takes Charge

by Diana Kimpton

Illustrated by Lizzie Finlay

Hyperion Paperbacks for Children
New York

For Heather, with love
—L.F.

First published in the United Kingdom in 2006 as
The Pony-Mad Princess: Princess Ellie Saves the Day
by Usborne Publishing Ltd.
Based on an original concept by Anne Finnis
Text copyright © 2006 by Diana Kimpton and Anne Finnis
Illustrations copyright © 2006 by Lizzie Finlay

Printed in the United States of America
First U.S. edition, 2007
1 3 5 7 9 10 8 6 4 2

This book is set in 14.5-point Nadine Normal.

ISBN-13: 978-14231-0617-3
ISBN-10: 1-4231-0617-2

Visit www.hyperionbooksforchildren.com

Chapter 1

"That's eighteen for me, seventeen for you," announced Princess Ellie as she wrote the score on the blackboard in the tack room. "I'm winning."

"Only for now," said her best friend, Kate. "I haven't had my turn yet."

"Here's your question, Kate," said Meg, the palace groom. "What's the name of the soft part on the bottom of a horse's foot?"

Kate grinned. "That's an easy one. It's the 'frog.'"

Ellie changed the score. "Okay, eighteen all. We're even now."

Meg peered out of the window. "The rain's stopped, and it's getting late. We'd better make this the last round of the quiz."

"Make it a hard one," said Ellie.

"I'll have to," Meg replied. "You've both gotten all the questions right so far." She paused thoughtfully for a moment. Then she said, "I have one. Suppose you found a pony

Kate Ellie

18

18

trying to bite at his stomach and looking around at his sides with a worried expression. What would be the matter?"

"Colic!" cried Ellie.

Meg nodded. "And for a bonus point, what should you do in that situation?" she asked.

Ellie hesitated. She'd never seen a pony with colic, and she hoped she never would. If she did, she knew she'd ask Meg for help, but that obviously wasn't the answer to the question. "I think I'd call the vet," she suggested.

"That's a good answer," replied Meg. "Colic can be serious—you don't want to take any chances."

Kate updated the score on the board. "You have twenty now," she said. "If I get both parts of my question right, it'll be a tie."

Meg handed her a few small pieces of something sticky. "Do you know what these are?"

Kate stared at the pieces carefully. She rolled them between her fingers and held them up to her nose to smell them. "Are they oats?" she asked.

"That's right," said Meg. "Now, for that bonus point, can you tell me what you must always do to oats before you put them in a mash for a pony?"

"I know, I know," squealed Ellie. She could hardly resist blurting out the answer.

"Don't tell me!" said Kate. She tapped thoughtfully on her teeth with a fingernail. She stared at her feet and then at the ceiling. Then she stared at the blackboard, as if she hoped the answer would miraculously appear on it. Eventually she admitted, "It's on the tip of my tongue, but I can't remember."

"Don't worry," said Meg. "Let's see if Ellie really knows."

Ellie felt very pleased with herself. "You have to soak them in hot water for a long time before you feed the mash to ponies."

"Of course," cried Kate. "How could I forget that! If you don't soak the oats, they could clump up and the pony could choke on them."

"Well done, both of you," said Meg.

"You're the winner, Ellie. I'm really impressed by how much you've both learned since I came to work at the royal stable."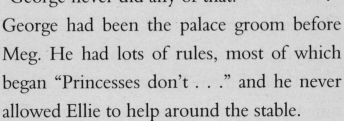

"That's only because you've taught us tons of stuff about pony care," laughed Ellie. "George never did any of that."

George had been the palace groom before Meg. He had lots of rules, most of which began "Princesses don't . . ." and he never allowed Ellie to help around the stable.

"I'm glad you're here now, Meg," said Kate. "It's so much fun to hang out at the stable when you're around."

"But it won't be much fun if I get in trouble for making you both late," added Meg.

"Do you have time to check the ponies' water before you go?"

"Of course we do," said Kate. "Grandma won't have my dinner ready yet." Kate's grandmother was the palace cook.

The yard was still wet from the rain that had sent the three of them scurrying into the tack room earlier. Ellie was glad to have her Wellington boots as she splashed through the puddles on the way to the tap. She filled

a bucket and used it to top off the water container in Sundance's stall. The chestnut pony nuzzled her shoulder as she worked. Ellie paused and stroked his glossy neck, delighting in the warm smell of horse mingled with the scent of fresh straw.

Rainbow looked out of her stall to see what was happening. Ellie ran her fingers through the pony's gray mane as she peeked over the door to check the water. Rainbow hadn't touched it yet. The container was still full to the brim.

Moonbeam's wasn't. It was half empty. Ellie

had to get another bucket to fill it up. As soon as she'd finished, the palomino pony plunged her cream-colored nose into the water and blew bubbles. Ellie laughed as Moonbeam shook her head, tossing her snow-white mane in all directions.

When Ellie went back outside, she saw Kate coming out of the large stall shared by Starlight and her foal, Angel. The other ponies were all Ellie's, but Angel wasn't— she belonged to Kate. "Have you checked on Shadow yet?" Ellie asked.

Kate nodded. "The silly old thing had knocked his water over. But I've filled it up again."

"Thanks to both of you," said Meg, as she stepped out of Gypsy's stable. She gave her gray thoroughbred a pat on the neck and added, "You've saved me some extra work. Would you girls be interested in a jumping lesson tomorrow?"

"That would be awesome!" cried Ellie.

"I'll wait for you in the yard after school," Meg promised.

When Ellie and Kate ran down to the stable for their lesson the next day, however, there was no sign of Meg at all. She had completely disappeared.

Chapter 2

"Meg?" called Ellie. "Where are you? Kate and I are here for our jumping lesson." But there was no reply. Meg was nowhere to be found, and all the stalls were empty, too.

"The ponies must still be out in the field," said Kate. "That's strange. Meg's usually brought them in by now, especially if we're going to have a lesson."

Ellie felt a nagging fear in the pit of her

stomach. Meg had promised to be there, and she always kept her promises. What could have happened to make her change her plans?

"Maybe she left us a message," suggested Kate. "Grandma always does if she's not going to be there when I get home from school." The girls ran over to the tack room and peered inside. To their disappointment, there was no letter on the table and no message written on the blackboard. Then Ellie noticed that those weren't the only things that weren't there. Gypsy's saddle wasn't on its rack, and neither was his bridle.

She breathed a sigh of relief. "It's all right," she explained. "Meg just went for a ride. She'll probably be back soon."

"I hope so," said Kate. "Let's get ready for

our lesson while we're waiting."

They got two halters from the tack room
and headed for the paddock.

Five of the six ponies watched them walk
up to the gate. Only Shadow, the Shetland,
took no notice. The greedy little pony was
too busy eating.

The girls rounded up Moonbeam and Sundance and led them back to the yard. Then they tied the ponies up and started to groom them. As Ellie brushed the mud from Moonbeam's legs, she listened hopefully for the sound of Gypsy's hooves along the bridle path. But no such sound came.

Half an hour later, both ponies were spotlessly clean. Kate finished oiling Sundance's feet and stood up. "I'm worried," she admitted. "Meg's never been this late before. Something must have happened."

Ellie nodded in agreement. "I think we should go and look for her," she suggested.

They put on the ponies' saddles and bridles as quickly as they could. Then Ellie swung herself onto Moonbeam's back while Kate mounted Sundance. As soon as they were ready, they clattered out of the yard.

It was only when they got outside that Ellie realized how difficult their search would be. "We have no idea which way Meg went," she groaned. "She could be anywhere in the palace grounds, and they're huge."

"Let's start by going up this trail," said

Kate. "She almost always goes this way. Maybe we'll find a clue or something to help us."

They rode slowly, looking carefully for any hint of Meg's whereabouts. But they didn't find one. Even if she had ridden in that direction, there was no way to tell if she had gone on into the deer park or turned through one of the gates.

"It's hopeless," sighed Ellie, when they reached the end of the trail. "We might as well go back. We're not doing any good out here." She tried to turn Moonbeam around to face the way they had come. But the palomino pony refused to move. Instead, she raised her head and whinnied loudly.

At first, Ellie was confused by her pony's behavior. Then, as the noise died away, she heard another, much fainter call. Somewhere in the distance, a horse was answering.

"It's Gypsy!" she yelled, pointing in the direction the sound had come from. "He's over there."

"That's the end of the cross-country course," said Kate. "Let's go!"

The two girls pushed their ponies into a gallop and raced across the open grass toward the trees that hid the wooden jumps. Normally, Ellie loved riding fast, but today she was too worried to enjoy it. She leaned low over Moonbeam's neck, trying to spot Gypsy.

They soon found the gray thoroughbred standing all alone beside the last jump. He couldn't come to meet them—his reins were tangled in a thornbush.

"That explains why he didn't run home,"

said Kate. "I wonder how long he's been here."

"And I wonder what's happened to Meg," added Ellie, her mouth dry with fear.

She jumped down from Moonbeam's back, passed the reins to Kate, and walked slowly around to the other side of the jump.

Upturned clumps of dirt in the grass showed where Gypsy must have lost his footing as he approached the wooden poles.

At the base of the fence lay a crumpled figure. As Ellie got closer, she got a sinking feeling in her stomach when she saw who it was. It was Meg—and she wasn't moving.

Chapter 3

"Meg! Are you all right?" cried Ellie, running over to where Meg lay with one leg twisted awkwardly. As Ellie crouched down, she tried desperately to remember everything she'd been taught about first aid. The only thing that came to mind was something about putting vinegar on wasp stings, or was that for bee stings? Whichever it was, it did not matter. Meg's injuries were far worse than a bee sting or a wasp sting.

Suddenly, Meg's eyes fluttered open. "Don't move me," she whispered, in a voice so soft that Ellie could barely hear it. "Go and get help."

Ellie was relieved to be told what to do. "She needs a doctor," she shouted, as she ran back to Kate. "And it's up to us to get one."

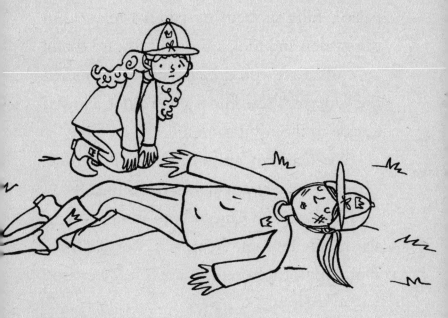

"You go," declared Kate. "Moonbeam's faster than Sundance, and one of us should stay here with Meg."

Ellie knew that Kate was right, so she jumped onto the palomino's back and raced away. She went as fast as she could, galloping over the grass and slowing only to a fast trot on the stony paths. As she approached the palace, Ellie spotted her parents relaxing in the garden and took a shortcut toward them.

"What are you doing, Aurelia?" shouted the Queen. "You know you're not allowed to ride in the royal garden."

"We need an ambulance!" yelled Ellie. "There's been an accident. Meg's hurt."

The King and Queen both jumped up in alarm. Neither of them was worried now about hoofprints on the grass. They were too busy asking Ellie where Meg was and organizing the help she needed. Soon, Higginbottom, the butler, was running to get the Range Rover, and the wail of a distant siren announced that the ambulance was coming.

Ellie didn't ask what she should do, in case someone told her to stay out of the way. She was determined to ride back to Meg to find out how she was doing. She needed to help Gypsy, too. After all, she and Kate were the only ones who knew how to look after him. It was up to them to bring him home.

She rode slowly now, giving Moonbeam time to cool down. By the time she reached the scene of the accident, the Range Rover and the ambulance were already there. Kate was standing with the King and Queen, watching with concern as Meg was carried into the waiting ambulance on a stretcher. She looked pale and in pain, but she managed to smile weakly at the girls.

Ellie waved at her as the ambulance doors slammed shut and the vehicle set off on its bumpy journey across the deer park. Then she rode over to Gypsy, jumped down from her saddle, and started to untangle the gray horse's reins from the thornbush. Gypsy whickered gently and nuzzled Ellie's shoulder.

"He looks pleased to have some attention," said Kate, as she ran over to help. "I was concentrating so hard on Meg that I forgot to talk to him."

"It's a good thing we're here," said Ellie, stroking the horse's velvety neck. "Everyone else is too busy to think about him." She pulled the reins free and sorted out Gypsy's stirrups so they wouldn't bang on his sides.

"I hope he'll be happy being led from Moonbeam. He's much too big for me to ride."

Ellie swung herself up into Moonbeam's saddle and tried to figure out a sensible way to hold her own reins as well as Gypsy's. She had never led a horse before while she was riding, so she was relieved that the gray thoroughbred walked calmly beside her when she set off. She was even more relieved when they arrived safely back at the stable.

The sight of the deserted yard brought home the seriousness of what had happened. Ellie blinked back tears as she remembered how Meg looked on the stretcher. Was she going to be all right? And would she ever be well enough to come back?

Chapter 4

Kate looked as miserable as Ellie felt. "The stable doesn't feel right without Meg," she sighed.

"I know," replied Ellie. "I already miss her so much." She sniffed loudly and wiped her eyes with the back of her hand. Then she forced herself to calm down and added, "I'm sure Meg wouldn't want us to sit around moping. The ponies need us. We've got to look after them by ourselves now."

They tied up Moonbeam, Sundance, and Gypsy in the yard and took off their saddles and bridles. Then they set to work putting down thick, straw beds in all the stalls, stuffing nets with hay, and filling all the water containers.

When everything was ready, they got the other ponies from the field and settled them in their stalls. The girls were just carrying the feed bowls around when the Queen walked into the yard.

"You've been very busy," she remarked.

"We're nearly finished," said Ellie. "We did everything all by ourselves."

The Queen smiled. "Meg would be proud of you for doing so well."

At the mention of Meg's name, Ellie couldn't hold back her tears any longer. They poured down her face as she asked, "Is she going to be all right?"

"It will be awful if she's not," wailed Kate.

"Don't worry," said the Queen, as she kneeled down and gave both girls a hug. "Meg will be fine, thanks to your rescue

mission. But she will have to stay in the hospital for a while."

Ellie sniffed loudly. "Can we see her?" she asked.

"Of course you can," replied the Queen. She produced a lace-trimmed hankie and dried Ellie's tears. "Your father and I are visiting her this evening, so you can come with us. The rules say only two visitors at a time, but I'm sure they can make an exception for a princess and her best friend."

An hour later, Ellie and Kate stepped out of the royal car and followed the King and Queen into the hospital. Neither of the girls was wearing her riding clothes anymore. Kate had washed away the dust from the stable and put on a white top and purple skirt.

Ellie had showered, too. She was wearing a frilly pink dress and her best tiara. In her hand, she clutched a bunch of flowers she had picked from the palace garden for Meg.

She had never been in a hospital before and was surprised to find it wasn't like the ones she saw on TV. There were no doctors rushing up and down the corridors, pushing

patients on stretchers and shouting orders. The only person in the entrance hall when they arrived was a janitor washing the floor.

"Can you please tell us the way to Buttercup Ward?" asked the King.

The janitor looked up from his work, saw the royal family, and dropped his mop in astonishment. He bowed low and mumbled, "Third floor, on the right, Your Majesties."

Ellie and her parents stepped into the

elevator with Kate and pressed the button for the third floor. The doors slid shut, a distant motor hummed, and the elevator moved slowly upward. By the time they stepped out on the third floor, news of their visit had spread throughout the hospital.

The corridor was lined with staff and patients eager to see the royal visitors. Some curtsied, some waved, and some just stared in wide-eyed curiosity.

"I feel like a goldfish in a bowl, with everyone looking at me," said Kate.

"So do I," agreed Ellie. "But I'm used to it."

As they arrived

in Buttercup Ward, the hospital director rushed up to them. He looked flustered and was hastily straightening his tie. "Welcome, Your Majesties," he declared, as he gave a deep bow. Then he launched into a well-rehearsed speech that Ellie suspected he used on all special occasions. "It is a great honor to have you here. As a token of our esteem, please allow me to present you with . . ."

His voice trailed away as he realized he didn't have anything to give them. Then he grabbed a bunch of flowers from the vase by the nearest bed and thrust the dripping stems into the Queen's hands.

The old lady in the bed glowered at him. "Those are mine," she grumbled.

"And very beautiful they are, too," said the Queen. She carefully put the flowers

back where they belonged and dabbed her
hand dry with her hankie.

The hospital director looked embarrassed
and smiled at Ellie. "It's delightful to have
you here, too, Princess Aurelia."

Ellie waved her own bunch of flowers

under his nose. "It's all right," she said. "I've already got some." She peered past him, spotted Meg lying on a bed in the corner of the ward, and ran over to join her.

Meg looked pale and tired. Her face was scratched, and one leg was in a cast.

But, to Ellie's great delight, she was well enough to smile at her visitors. "Here come my rescuers," she laughed.

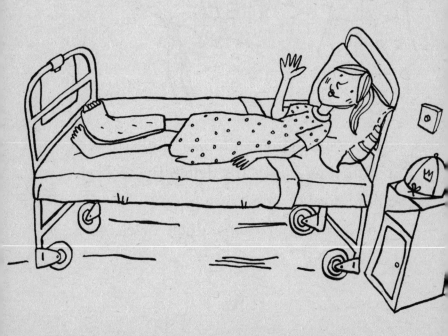

"It was Gypsy and Moonbeam who saved you," explained Kate. "We'd never have found you if they hadn't whinnied to each other."

"I'm glad Gypsy did something right," said the Queen. "Didn't he cause the accident?"

"It wasn't his fault," replied Meg. "I should have realized how slippery the ground would be after yesterday's rain."

"Are you going to be all right?" asked Ellie, handing Meg the flowers.

Meg lifted them to her nose and sniffed. "I already feel better now that I've got these." Then she smiled and added, "Don't worry. I'm going to be fine. But I'm afraid I won't be back at the stable for a while. I've broken my leg, and it will take several weeks to heal."

"You're not to worry about anything," said the King. "We can ask George to come back. Although he's retired, I'm sure he'd be happy to run the stable until you're better."

Ellie stared at her father in horror. She didn't want George to come back. She loved being free to help out in the stable and ride her ponies whenever she liked. George and his rules would spoil *everything*.

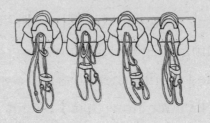

Chapter 5

"No!" cried Ellie in alarm. "We don't need George. Kate and I can look after the stable by ourselves."

The Queen shook her head. "It's too much for you to handle. You're both too young—you can't possibly know enough about taking care of ponies."

"We do," declared Ellie and Kate in unison. They both looked pleadingly at Meg.

Surely she could understand why George coming back would be such a bad idea.

To Ellie's relief, Meg came to their rescue. "The girls do know a great deal," she explained. "They help me all the time, and I'm really impressed by the amount they've learned about pony care."

Unfortunately, the King had thought of another problem. "Looking after six ponies and a horse is hard work, Aurelia. Meg is busy all day long, but you have lessons to go to, and so does Kate."

"I'll get up really early," Ellie promised.

"So will I," agreed Kate. "We can do most of the work before school and then finish the rest of it afterward."

"Please, please, *please*," begged Ellie. "I know we can take charge of the stable, if you just give us the chance."

Her parents looked unconvinced. "I still don't think you realize how much work is involved," said the King.

"Perhaps you should let them find out," suggested Meg. She winked at Ellie and added, "It would be a very good lesson in responsibility."

The Queen patted her husband on the arm. "That's true, my dear. Responsibility is a very important thing for a princess to understand."

"I suppose so," the King reluctantly agreed. Then he turned to Ellie and said in a serious voice, "You and Kate can have your chance. But if running the stable starts to affect your school work, I will send for George immediately."

The next morning, Ellie's alarm clock buzzed loudly at half past five. Ellie was already awake.

She had tossed and turned all night, thinking of everything that had to be done at the stable. She didn't want to make a mistake.

She pulled on her riding clothes and raced through the silent, sleeping palace. Her heart thumped with excitement as she stepped outside and ran over to the stable. This was a real adventure. She'd never been to the yard so early before. It lay still and quiet, waiting for the day to begin.

Sundance put his head out of his stall and whickered a welcome. Gypsy looked out, too. A wisp of straw clung to one of his ears, and his face looked ghostly white in the gray light of dawn.

Kate arrived a few minutes later, and the two girls set to work with enthusiasm. They started by giving out the morning feed. While the ponies munched their breakfast, the girls collected the empty hay nets from the stalls and refilled them in the barn. Then they turned Gypsy and the ponies loose in the field to graze, and started mucking out the stable.

Without Meg's help, everything took much longer than they expected. By the time they had to go back to the palace for breakfast, they still had two stalls left to clean, and the yard looked a complete mess, with straw and manure all over it. But there was no time to do any more work that morning, even though they were both worried about their very slow progress. As soon as they finished breakfast, Kate had to go to school, and Ellie had lessons with her governess, Miss Stringle.

The girls were used to finding everything clean and tidy when they went to the stable after school. But today was different—today the yard still looked as bad as when they'd left it. They had to finish the morning's work before they could start putting straw beds down in all the stalls and refilling the water containers. Then they had to bring the ponies in from the field and groom them all.

Gypsy took a long time to clean up. His gray coat was covered with stains, and he wasn't as cooperative as the ponies when the girls tried to clean out his feet. Each time Ellie picked up one of his hooves, the horse leaned all of his weight on that leg. Ellie had to work fast, before she was forced to put it down again.

There was no time to go for a ride. The whole afternoon was filled with work and, even then, they didn't manage to clean the saddles and bridles they had used the day before.

Kate sighed as they topped off the water containers before they went home. "I never realized before how hard Meg works," she groaned. "I'm worn out."

"So am I," agreed Ellie. "I hope it gets easier once we get used to it." She felt completely exhausted. Her arms were so tired that she could hardly lift the bucket of water. She had a blister on her hand from all of the sweeping, and her back ached from all of the lifting.

That night Ellie had no trouble sleeping. She was so tired that she didn't even dream. The problem came in the morning when she had to wake up.

Chapter 6

Ellie groaned loudly as the alarm clock buzzed. She switched it off and pulled the covers over her head. Then she remembered that she had to get up. The ponies needed her, and she didn't want George to come back.

She climbed out of bed, dragged herself into the bathroom, and splashed cold water on her face. That helped her to wake up, so she put on her riding clothes and headed for the stable.

Kate was waiting for her in the yard.

She was sitting on an upturned bucket, with her hair uncombed. "Are you feeling as tired as I am?" she yawned.

"Definitely," replied Ellie, trying not to yawn, too. "We'd better get started. There's a lot to do."

The day before, running the stable had felt like an exciting adventure. Today it didn't. It was just sheer hard work—carrying feed, filling hay nets, and mucking out stalls. Although Ellie enjoyed taking the ponies to the field, her aching back protested every time she pushed the wheelbarrow, and the blister on her hand hurt as she swept out the stable.

The girls were so tired that everything took even longer than it had the day before. There were still lots of chores left to do when they had to go back to the palace. Ellie considered staying longer, but she knew she couldn't risk being late for her lessons.

Back in her pink bedroom, she looked longingly at her four-poster bed. A nap would have been wonderful, but there wasn't time. Instead, she stood in a hot shower to relieve her aching muscles. Then she dressed for her lessons and ran to the dining room for breakfast.

"Looking after the stable is certainly

giving you an appetite," said the Queen, as Ellie started on her third slice of toast.

"Mmmm," nodded Ellie, with her mouth full. She'd spread the marmalade extra thick in the hope that the extra sugar would give her lots of energy.

The King looked at his watch. "Hurry up, Aurelia. It's time for your lessons. Remember what I said about your school work."

Ellie didn't need reminding. The threat of George was never far from her mind. She gulped down the last of the toast, drank the rest of the orange juice from her crystal glass, and ran to the schoolroom. On the way, she licked the sticky remnants of the marmalade from her fingers—there wasn't time to wash her hands.

Miss Stringle was already at her desk when Ellie arrived. She didn't look pleased at being kept waiting. "Sit down at once, Your Highness," she said sternly. "We'll start the morning with some math problems to wake up your brain."

Ellie's brain was as tired as the rest of her body. It didn't want to be woken up, and it certainly didn't want to do any math. Although she tried hard to concentrate, she kept making silly mistakes.

"Do pay attention, Princess Aurelia," said Miss Stringle. "If one princess can kiss three frogs, how many frogs can three princesses kiss?"

Ellie wrinkled up her nose in disgust.

She didn't like the idea of kissing frogs at all.

"Six?" she guessed.

"No, no, no," said Miss Stringle. "It's three times three, and that is . . . ?" She paused dramatically, obviously waiting for the answer.

Ellie bit her lip nervously. "Nine?" she ventured.

"At last," sighed Miss Stringle. "Now that you've finally gotten one right, we'll move on to geography." She pointed at a map of the world pinned up on the wall. "Please point to Andirovia, and tell me about it."

Ellie stood up confidently. She knew the answer this time because her friend, Prince John, was from Andirovia, and he always enjoyed telling Ellie about his homeland. As she picked out the right place on the map, she said, "Andirovia has lots of mountains. The weather is very different from here. In the winter, there is lots of snow."

For the first time that morning, Miss Stringle looked pleased. "Well done, Princess Aurelia. You've learned that well." She pointed at another much larger country. "Now I'm going to teach you about Sanbarosa."

That name sounds very familiar, thought Ellie. Then she remembered. That was where Princess Clara was from. She had met Clara not too long before, when she had gone on summer vacation.

Ellie sat down again, hoping the Sanbarosa geography lesson would be easy. To her delight, Miss Stringle switched on the video. Watching that would take no effort at all.

The voice coming from the television screen announced, "Sanbarosa, land of sun, sea, and sheep."

It was one of the most beautiful places Ellie had ever seen. A golden sun blazed down on pure, white sand. Clear blue waves lapped gently on the shore.

Ellie yawned and made herself more comfortable. Gradually, she stopped listening to the droning voice on the video and imagined herself lying on that gorgeous beach.

The more she thought about it, the more relaxed she became. Her eyes closed, her head nodded, and she fell fast asleep.

"Aurelia!" roared the King.

Ellie jumped up with a start. Her eyes snapped open, and, for a brief moment, she couldn't remember where she was. Then she saw Miss Stringle and her father. They both looked very angry. "Oh, no," she groaned, as she realized what had happened.

"See?" said Miss Stringle, pointing accusingly at Ellie. "She was even snoring."

"I was not!" protested Ellie, but the King kept looking at her sternly.

"Do you remember what I said would happen if running the stable affected your schoolwork?" he asked.

Ellie nodded miserably. "You said you'd send for George."

"And I always keep my word," said the King. "He'll be here later this afternoon."

Chapter 7

Ellie told Kate the news when they met in the yard after school. To her surprise, her friend wasn't as miserable about it as she had expected.

"I've been tired all day," Kate explained. "Looking after all the ponies is much harder than I thought. I don't think we could've managed on our own until Meg came back."

Deep inside, Ellie knew Kate was right.

"We do need help," she admitted. "But George will take over and stop us from helping to look after the ponies. I just know he will."

Kate looked thoughtful. "But maybe he won't, if we can prove how good we are."

"I don't think that will make any difference," said Ellie. "George was very set in his ways."

"Maybe he's more relaxed now that he's retired," suggested Kate. "It must be worth a try."

"I guess so," replied Ellie, her voice still tinged with doubt. She glanced around at the overflowing wheelbarrows, the

messy stalls, and the untidy yard.

"Let's make sure everything is perfect when he arrives."

Their plan filled them with new energy. As quickly as they could, they finished mucking out the stable and put clean straw down in all the stalls. Then they tied up the bulging nets of hay, filled all the water containers, and brought the ponies in from the field.

Ellie was just finishing sweeping the yard when George arrived. He looked older than she remembered him. The small amount of hair left on his head was gray, and he walked more slowly than before.

"Hello, George," she said. "We brought the ponies in for you."

The old groom said, "Thank you kindly,

Your Highness." Then he reached out and took the broom away from her. "You won't be needing that anymore. Princesses don't sweep yards when I'm in charge."

Ellie glared at him angrily. Then she glanced at Kate and whispered, "I told you so."

Kate took a step toward George. "I could do it if you like," she suggested. "I'm not a princess."

"And who might you be?" asked George.

"Kate is the cook's granddaughter," Ellie explained. "She's my best friend, too, and she owns Angel."

George looked puzzled. "Who, may I ask, is Angel?"

"She's Starlight's foal," explained Ellie. She'd forgotten that so much had happened since George retired.

George raised his eyebrows questioningly. "And Starlight is . . . ?"

"My new pony," said Ellie, proudly. "Come and meet her." She led the way to the large stall that the bay mare shared with her foal.

George looked slightly upset as he walked slowly beside her. "No one told me about extra ponies," he grumbled. "That's extra work for me." But his face softened when he saw Starlight and Angel standing side by side, knee deep in straw. "They're beautiful.

That mare's a bit heavy for a princess, but she's my kind of pony."

His approval of Starlight made Ellie feel friendlier toward him. "We'll show you around, if you like," she offered.

"I'm sure I can manage, Your Highness. I've worked here long enough to know where everything is." As if to prove his point, he marched across the yard to the feed room.

The girls followed him inside and watched as he lifted the lids on the storage bins to check what was inside. He nodded as he looked at the barley and chaff, but raised his eyebrows again when he looked into the third bin. "Newfangled nonsense," he muttered.

"They're just oats," said Ellie. "We use them to make mash—Moonbeam's favorite. Oh, but you have to soak them in hot

water first, so the ponies don't choke."

"I know, I know," said George, firmly. "Princesses don't need to worry their heads about that sort of thing." He shut the lid, left the feed room, and walked over to investigate the tack room.

Kate was about to follow him inside, but Ellie stopped her. She remembered that one of George's rules was "princesses don't go in tack rooms." So the two girls stood outside and peered through the open doorway.

George muttered to himself as he looked around the room. He cleaned the blackboard, tidied up a pile of pony magazines, and looked disapprovingly at Moonbeam's dirty bridle. Then he turned to Ellie and asked, "Which pony would you like to ride tomorrow?"

"Rainbow," she replied. "And it's Kate's turn to ride Moonbeam."

He carefully wrote both names on the board. "Tomorrow's Saturday, and it makes sense to ride in the morning before it gets hot. I'll have both ponies ready at eleven."

"You don't have to do that," said Ellie, quickly. "Meg's taught me a lot about pony care. I can get them ready myself now, and I can help with the mucking out."

George stared at her disapprovingly. "There's no need, Your Highness. I can cope very well on my own. Princesses don't help at the stable when I'm in charge."

Then he glanced at Kate and added, "And that goes for you, too."

Chapter 8

Ellie enjoyed being able to lie in bed the following morning. But she didn't enjoy being separated from her ponies. Usually she spent the whole of Saturday at the stable. George's return had changed that completely.

She met Kate in the royal garden after breakfast. They were both already in their riding clothes, although they couldn't ride until later. As there was nothing else to do until eleven, they decided to go for a walk.

"It's not fair," grumbled Ellie, as they wandered along the bank of the stream. "I'm really missing the ponies."

"So am I," moaned Kate. She threw a stick into the rushing water and watched as it was swept away. "It's silly making us schedule our ride instead of letting us just turn up at the stable whenever we're ready."

"At least we can make sure it's a good ride," said Ellie. "Let's go along my favorite trail in the forest—the one where the ponies like to splash through the stream."

"Yes! And after that, let's go to the top of that hill," suggested Kate, pointing to the other side of the deer park. "I love it up there. We can have a long canter across the grass."

Planning their ride cheered the girls up. By the time they arrived at the stable, they had worked out every detail. At exactly eleven o'clock, they walked into the yard and found that George had kept his promise. He was waiting for them with Rainbow and Moonbeam. Both ponies were saddled and bridled, ready to go out.

Unfortunately, they weren't the only ones that were ready. To Ellie's dismay, she noticed that George had saddled Gypsy, too, and there was only one possible reason he would have done that.

"You don't need to come with us," she protested.

"Yes, I do, Your Highness," replied George. He tightened Rainbow's girth and held the pony still while Ellie mounted. "I'm the groom, and that's part of my job. Princesses don't go riding by themselves when I'm in charge."

He glanced at Kate and added, "And that goes for you, too." Then he helped her onto Moonbeam and fussed with the stirrups, making sure they were the right length.

When he was sure that both Ellie and Kate were ready to go, he led Gypsy over to the mounting block and used it to swing

himself onto the gray thoroughbred's back.

Ellie found it strange to see him riding Meg's horse. "I'm surprised you didn't bring Captain with you," she said. George had owned Captain for as long as she could remember, and he'd taken the big, black horse with him when he'd left the stable.

George shook his head and smiled. "It wouldn't be fair," he explained. "My old

Captain is retired, like me. He's gotten used to doing nothing. It wouldn't be fair to make him work hard again."

As they rode out of the yard, Ellie wondered if the same were true of George. Now that she had tried running the stable, she realized what a huge amount of work it was. Maybe it was too much for one old man to manage by himself. That would explain why Rainbow still had tangles in her mane. It looked as if the pony hadn't been brushed at all.

The ride George took them on was not at all like the one the girls had planned. They didn't splash through the stream. They did not ride to the top of the hill or canter across the grass. They just walked idly along tree-lined paths, and had an occasional slow trot.

It was the quietest ride Ellie had been on in a long while. But it was still wonderful to be on Rainbow's back, feeling the gentle rhythm of her walk and watching her flick her ears as she listened to all the sounds around them. Ellie couldn't bear the thought that this might be the only contact she had with her ponies that day. She had to do something to stop George from spoiling all her fun.

When they got back to the yard, the two girls jumped off Moonbeam and Rainbow. George slid more slowly down from Gypsy's back. He looked stiff and tired after the ride.

Ellie spotted her chance. Before he could stop her, she led Rainbow swiftly toward her stall. "Don't worry, George," she called. "I'll unsaddle her."

She led the pony inside and looked around in surprise. Although the yard looked clean and organized, the stable didn't. Last night's hay net hung empty on the wall. Bits of hay floated in the water left over from the previous night, and the floor was still covered with dirty straw and manure.

George met her at the door, as she stepped out carrying Rainbow's saddle and bridle. He took them from her firmly, looking slightly flustered, probably because she'd seen how behind he was with the work. "There's no need for you to help," he insisted. "I can cope. I'm just a little out of practice, that's all."

"But we like helping," said Kate.

"That's got nothing to do with it," said George. "Looking after the stable is my job. It's up to me to do it." He let them schedule another ride for Sunday morning. Then he hurried them out of the yard.

"I'm worried," said Ellie, as they walked slowly back to the palace.

"About what?" asked Kate.

"George hadn't groomed the ponies very well," explained Ellie. "And he hasn't mucked out the stalls, either. I think he's too old to manage on his own, and, if George can't cope, the ponies are going to suffer."

Now Kate looked worried, too. "Perhaps you should tell your parents," she suggested.

Ellie shook her head. "They won't believe me. They never do. They'll say we're imagining it because we don't want George to be here."

"Do you think we are?" asked Kate.

Her words made Ellie think carefully. She didn't want to get George into trouble if there was nothing wrong. But if there was, she wanted to make sure the ponies were safe. Surely there was some way they could discover the truth.

Chapter 9

"Are you sure this is going to work?" said Kate, when the two girls met in the royal garden after lunch.

"Of course I am," replied Ellie. She held up the binoculars that Miss Stringle made her use during bird-watching lessons. "We can watch George all afternoon through these to see how he's managing. Then, if we're still worried, I'll

have some evidence for Mom and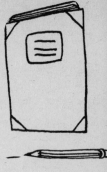
Dad." She looked questioningly at
Kate. "You did remember the
notebook, didn't you?"

"Yes," laughed her friend. "And the pen-
cil and some sticky buns. Grandma thought
we might get hungry."

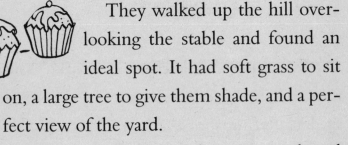 They walked up the hill over-
looking the stable and found an
ideal spot. It had soft grass to sit
on, a large tree to give them shade, and a perfect view of the yard.

They each took turns keeping watch and
writing down everything they saw in the
notebook. The old groom worked slowly but
steadily all afternoon without a break. He
mucked out the stable, put down fresh bed-
ding, and swept the yard. By the time he

brought the ponies in from the field, he looked exhausted. His shoulders were slumped, and his feet dragged as he walked.

Ellie felt sorry for him. She knew how tired he must feel. She watched until all the ponies were safely in their stalls. Then she passed the binoculars to Kate while she ate the last of the buns.

When she'd swallowed the last mouthful, she asked, "What's he doing now?"

"He's giving out the feed," said Kate.

Ellie kneeled beside her. "Can you see what he's giving them?"

"No," said Kate. "The

feed bowls are too deep. I can't see what's in them."

"I hope he remembered Starlight's carrots," said Ellie. "She'll be miserable if she doesn't have those." The thought brought all her worries tumbling back. Watching from a distance wasn't good enough. "I can't bear not being there. I need to see for myself that everything's all right."

"So do I," said Kate. "If I don't say good night to Angel, she might think I don't love her anymore."

They picked up the binoculars and the notebook and scurried down the hillside. Then they crept quietly up to the stable and peered into the yard.

"We're in luck," whispered Ellie. George was sitting on a chair outside the tack room.

His head was slumped forward with his chin on his chest, and he was snoring gently.

Kate looked at the old groom nervously. "Maybe he's just dozing. If he is, he'll wake up as soon as he hears us."

"No, I don't think so," replied Ellie. "He looked so tired earlier. I bet he's fast asleep." But she still walked on tiptoe as she led the way into the yard.

First, they checked on Sundance. The chestnut pony flicked his ears forward when he saw them coming and nuzzled Ellie's shoulder lovingly. She gave him a peppermint and gently stroked his face.

"He looks fine," whispered Kate. "Maybe we've been worrying about nothing."

Suddenly, there was a very peculiar noise. It was a strange coughing sound, quite different from anything Ellie had ever heard before. She quickly ran to the next stall and peered over the door, searching for the source of the sound. Rainbow looked back at her, happily munching a wisp of hay. There was nothing wrong there.

The strange cough came again. This time Ellie realized who was making it. "It's Moonbeam," she cried. She raced toward the palomino pony's stall, with Kate close behind.

As soon as they opened the stable door, they realized something was dreadfully wrong. Moonbeam looked terrified. She was standing with her head and neck outstretched. She was coughing and struggling to swallow.

"What's wrong with her?" asked Kate, her eyes wide with alarm.

"I don't know," cried Ellie. Then she glanced down at the feed bowl and spotted the remains of some pony mash lying at the bottom of it.

A shiver of fear ran down her spine as she realized what must have happened. George had made some mash for Moonbeam, but he'd forgotten to soak the oats first. Now Moonbeam was in terrible danger.

Chapter 10

Ellie raced to the phone in the tack room, while Kate ran to check the other ponies. Neither of them worried about being quiet now. All that mattered was saving Moonbeam.

George woke up with a start and stared angrily at Ellie. "What's happening?" he asked.

"We've got to get the vet here quickly!"

she shouted. "Moonbeam's choking."

George's grumpiness immediately disappeared. "I'll call him," he said. "You go back to Moonbeam. Keep her calm, and make sure she doesn't eat or drink anything."

He vanished into the tack room, and Ellie rushed back to Moonbeam's stall. As she ran quickly across the yard, she repeated George's instructions to herself to help her remember them. It was only then she realized that, for the first time ever, George had asked her to help.

She found Moonbeam still looking as distressed as she had before. Ellie stroked the pony's neck soothingly. Then she quickly moved the feed bowl and water out of the pony's reach.

The sound of running feet outside the

stall announced Kate's return. She slipped quietly through the door and said, "All the others are fine. I don't think he gave them any mash."

"Thank goodness for that," said Ellie. She quickly explained George's instructions. Then she stroked Moonbeam's face again and softly whispered, "Don't be scared. It's okay. Everything's going to be all right." She tried to sound confident, but she didn't really feel it.

To Ellie's relief, the vet arrived a few minutes later. "It's your lucky day," he said. "I was just up the road seeing to a sick cow."

He opened a bag, took out a needle, and gave Moonbeam an injection. "That will make her relax so it's easier for the mash to go down." Then he pulled a long, flexible tube from his bag and explained, "I'm going to push this gently down her throat and put some water down it to clear away the blockage."

Moonbeam already looked calmer. Ellie wanted to stay with her, but the vet needed space to work. "You two girls have done a splendid job," he said. "But there's nothing more you can do for now. I'll call you back when I'm finished."

Ellie stepped reluctantly into the yard and was relieved to see her parents waiting for her. They had heard that there was an emergency at the stable, and they had come immediately to find out what was happening.

The Queen gave Ellie a big hug. "Moonbeam's in good hands. The vet knows what he's doing."

Ellie knew that her mother was right, but she couldn't stop worrying. The minutes ticked by painfully slowly. The longer she waited, the more anxious she became.

Eventually, the door swung open, and the vet stepped out. To Ellie's relief, he was smiling broadly. "It's all okay now," he announced. "Moonbeam's going to be fine."

As if to prove the point, George led the palomino pony out into the yard. She looked like her normal self again.

"Thank you, thank you," squealed Ellie, as she threw her arms around Moonbeam's neck.

"Thank *you*," laughed the vet. "It was you who spotted the problem so quickly."

"And it was me who caused it," said George, sadly. "I made the mash for Moonbeam because you said she liked it. But I was so tired that I forgot all about soaking the oats." He turned to the King and bowed. "I'm very sorry, Your Majesty. I'm afraid I'm too old to run the stable. I will leave immediately, of course."

Ellie felt sorry for him. He hadn't wanted to hurt Moonbeam. He'd been trying to make her happy. "You don't have to go," she said. "You could stay and let us help."

"We can't run the stable without you," explained Kate. "And you can't manage all the work without us. But together we could make a good team."

"That's an excellent idea," said the King. He turned to George and asked, "Would you be happy with that, just until Meg comes back?"

George smiled. "It sounds like the perfect solution, Your Majesty," he replied. "Princesses seem good at helping." He glanced at Kate and added, with a smile, "And that goes for you, too."

Ellie grinned and hugged Moonbeam

again. She was still looking forward to Meg coming back, but at least life with George around was going to be much more fun from now on.

Collect all the books in this royally fun pony series!

by Diana Kimpton